T0015414

THE OTHER ONES

by Jamesie Fournier

illustrated by Toma Feizo Gas

INHABIT
MEDIA

Published by Inhabit Media Inc.

www.inhabitmedia.com

Inhabit Media Inc. (Iqaluit) P.O. Box 11125, Iqaluit, Nunavut, X0A 1H0

Editors: Neil Christopher and Kelly Ward
Art Director: Danny Christopher

ISBN: 978-1-77227-421-9

This project was made possible in part by the Government of Canada.

We acknowledge the support of the Canada Council for the Arts for our publishing
program.

Library and Archives Canada Cataloguing in Publication

Title: The other ones / by Jamesie Fournier ; illustrated by Toma Feizo Gas.
Names: Fournier, Jamesie, author. | Gas, Toma Feizo, 1979- illustrator.
Identifiers: Canadiana 20220440522 | ISBN 9781772274219 (hardcover)
Subjects: LCGFT: Short stories. | LCGFT: Horror fiction.
Classification: LCC PS8611.O87335 O84 2022 | DDC C813/.6—dc23

Printed in Canada

THE OTHER ONES

The Net 3

Before Dawn 38

Glossary of Inuktut Words 46

INHABIT
MEDIA

The Net

The mother and daughter had been going to the cabin every season since the daughter was a child. Originally, the cabin had belonged to the mother's mother, the girl's late grandmother. Here, the daughter had learned to fish and hunt from her mother, just as her mother had learned from hers. By the time the girl was ten, she could gut a fish just as easily as she could ride a bike. Now, at fourteen, her relationship with her mother was starting to change. She could feel herself drifting away and was not sure how she felt about it. Her mother had brought her out here hoping that she could ground herself once more before facing whatever life had in store for her next. They both wondered if this would be their last trip to the cabin together.

This winter, they snowmobiled across lake trails to the old cabin, dragging their large sleds, or *qamutiit*, behind them. As they rode, the mother scanned the horizon and marvelled at the forest. Winter cold defined the landscape, and, in the distance, she saw her mother's petite one-room cabin at the crest of a small island. Two wooden poles jutted out of the lake ice ahead of the cabin like long, skeletal fingers closing in on them. At twenty metres apart, these poles marked the end and the beginning of the fishing net the mother had set underneath the ice days before.

Once at the net, they took their ice chisels out of their qamutiit and chipped away at the base of the poles. The long, carved handles balanced the heft of the blades. At the end of each handle was laced a loop of string, which they would wrap around their wrists as they chipped at the ice. The mother called them the "Holy Shit" ropes, for when they would eventually break through the last layer of ice, their chisels would plunge startlingly into the lake like vicious harpoons. Thus, the expletive. The strings kept them attached and off the bottom of the lake. The daughter had learned this lesson the hard way. One winter, she was chipping away at the ice without having secured her string and, the moment she broke through, her chisel was swallowed by the lake. Wide eyed, she had stood mute and unbelieving, watching her chisel slowly disappear. That winter they went home early and empty handed.

Once through the ice, they pulled the wooden poles out of the water and dragged fistfuls of net onto the ice. As they pulled, the daughter could have sworn she heard a faint thudding in the distance. A knocking underneath the ice. She paused and held her breath, mesmerized, as she watched the waves swell and overflow the small, chipped hole. She snapped back when dark, slimy bodies began to pull out of the icy water. One by one, they untangled the fat-bellied fish and threw them into the snow. They were mostly jack and whitefish, but every so often a pickerel would catch their eye, and the mother and daughter would shoot each other a look. The daughter marvelled at the colours as the fish flowed from dark green to the white of their underbellies. She remembered her grandmother telling her that the colder the water, the fatter the fish would be, and with more fat came more flavour. The cold had seasoned them, made them more savoury.

"It looks like something tore the net down there pretty good!" the mother yelled as she studied the armful before her. "A big jack, maybe . . . or a beaver?" The mother sighed, frustrated. The daughter turned to the vicious hole ripped through the net's centre. It seemed like it had been attacked, rather than something simply being caught in it. The daughter imagined twisting and turning underwater, tangled and drowning. How awful it would be, tearing your way out. However, the realization that a torn net actually had fewer holes in it than it did before derailed her thinking and left her absently staring at the net. "Gonna have to fix this tonight," the mother groaned.

The daughter was not keen on staying up all night mending the old net. However, it meant they did not need to reset it tonight. Which was no small task—more holes would need to be dug, and then the net would need to be laced from hole to hole. A cold, wet, and messy job if there ever was one.

Besides, working with her hands eased her mind and helped her relax. Her stomach also held no objections as it grumbled at the thought of an early dinner.

The daughter brought in a fat pickerel, which she cleaned with ease. She carefully removed each cheek and popped them into her mouth like delicious scallops. Her mother, on the other hand, had a penchant for the eyes, which she quickly cut out with her *ulu*, claiming they tasted just like candy. Her daughter wrinkled her nose and they both laughed heartily. The daughter filleted the rest, which she dredged and fried in a cast-iron pan. The cabin filled with the aroma of crisp, golden fish, which they dipped in small dishes of mayonnaise and ate with deep, venting breaths.

After the net had been mended, the mother lay down in her bed while the daughter lit candles and stretched out on the sofa with a loop of string. She absently wove her fingers back and forth and practised the old string figures her grandmother had taught her way back when. She remembered how she and her grandmother used to duel each other. Starting from an open position, they would declare a figure and race to see who was fastest. Best two out of three. She didn't stand a chance against her grandma. The girl remembered her old, gnarled fingers bending with incredible speed and dexterity. Her eerie patterns always told a story. Swollen and cracked, her knuckles had spun more tales than the girl could remember. Her grandmother would fall into a trance and she would sit, mesmerized by the strings, and drift away. As the daughter lay on the couch, she wove her fingers while a cold breeze blew over the lake, curled about the cabin, and slid underneath the door. The candles guttered in the small room.

"Be careful what you're doing there, Missy," her mother uttered beneath thick covers. The daughter started at her mother's voice, thinking she had been asleep. "You remember

what your *anaanatsiaq* told you about them things. Shouldn't do them at night." She rolled in her bed. "S'bad luck. Everything's asleep."

The daughter took a moment and remembered. Her grandmother had been a superstitious woman. She had all sorts of rules that didn't quite add up. Forbidden organs that could not be eaten, certain trees she had to stay away from, which shoulder she should spit over . . . stuff like that. She remembered her once teaching her how to nail a shadow to the ground, but her mother had stepped in and said that had been quite enough education for one day. Her mother had dismissed a lot of what her grandmother had tried to teach her, and the daughter had felt the poorer for it. And now here her mother was, scolding her with those very lessons she had denied her. The irony was not lost on her.

9

"So, what if I do?" the daughter snapped, malcontent. Her mother groaned and sat up.

"You wake them up. The *Inuunngittut*, you remember, those Other Ones your anaanatsiaq loved to go on about?" She scoffed. "The Sleeping Ones. Inhuman. They come for you. Drag you under, hide you forever." The mother sighed. "You know, never to be found again. All that crap. Boy, she loved to scare me with those damn stories of hers." The mother rolled over. "But what do I know," she added over her shoulder before falling asleep.

The girl stared at the loop of string between her fingers. She remembered sitting on her grandmother's lap, listening to her tell a story. A story of angels. How they rose and fell between Heaven and Earth. There was a ladder that connected the two worlds, the spiritual and the physical, existence and eternity. She remembered her grandmother whispering to her, "All demons were once angels long, long ago, eh, my girl?" She remembered looking up at her and nodding. "How many came into our world on their ladder, huh? A door swings both ways, you know."

The daughter shook her head and looked dimly about the cabin. She squinted and saw her mother asleep in her corner bed and that the candles had burned down low. When she looked at her hands, she saw that her fingers were queerly laced together. A ladder stretched in between them as if muscle memory had possessed her, conjuring the bridge. Just then a gust of wind crashed the door open. The doorway filled with blowing snow. The daughter jumped to shut it. While she grasped at the door, the wind pushed back against her. She gritted her teeth and heaved, yet the door would not budge. Snow flew across and stung her face. Suddenly, her mother was beside her, yelling and throwing all her weight with her. The door slammed shut, thudding at the hinges.

"Lock it!" the mother yelled as frozen air screamed behind the door. The daughter reached and turned the bolt. Once it was locked, they leaned back against the door and gasped for air. The daughter brought a hand to her chest and stopped short when she saw the string dangling from her fingers. She quickly dropped her hands. Her mother gazed from her daughter's eyes to the string and back again. "Quit playing around," her mother groaned as she paced back to bed, "before you get us both killed." The daughter stared at the loop between her fingers, then flung it to the floor.

Both eventually fell asleep. The daughter twisted and turned while her mother slept unbothered. The daughter dreamed. She dreamed she was underwater, sinking underneath the ice, the current blue-black and emerald. Above, a round blemish began to clear on the underside of the ice. Muted thuds crashed as flecks of light began to seep through. Suddenly, a spear plunged through the ice into wet, green cold. A pillar of light descended. She turned her head and saw she was back in the cabin. The crack underneath the door shone bright. Water-logged and groaning with pressure, the door's hinges rattled and shook in place. The deadbolt twitched with every crash. Slipping. Just a matter of time. Underneath the water again, her throat tightened. Her lungs emptied. A silent certainty washed over her. The pillars of light fluttered beneath the waves. They crisscrossed and prismed into strings of light. Stitched together, a net—a ladder—was coming down, descending to her. Sinking, she kicked to reach the bottom rung, yet something pulled her back. She looked down and saw her foot tangled in seaweed. She shook her foot nervously and watched, horrified, as the leaves solidified into fingers that clawed about her ankle. Her gaze drifted down the drowned hand when suddenly two white, horrid eyes flashed open in the dark. They peered back at her, curiously She watched in terror as the hunger in those eyes jolted into life. The arm seized her and dragged her down sharply. The creature's nails dug into her flesh as she reached for the ladder. She screamed in pain, and it bubbled to the surface. The ladder shone brightly above her as she struggled to be free. Panicked, she looked down again and saw those silver-dollar eyes stare into her longingly. She stomped her heel into its darkened face and felt the creature's grip loosen as she pushed upwards. She grasped the bottom loop of string and immediately felt it pull her up toward the light. The horrid face faded into the darkness as the ice shattered above her into a multitude of light. As she breached the surface, her eyes froze in their sockets, splintering the bones beneath her skin.

She shot brusquely awake, gasping. She looked to the door. It hung to one side, violated like a torn fingernail. She turned and yelled for her mother, yet nothing came out. Her mother slept undisturbed, peacefully in dreams. The daughter turned back to the door and immediately stopped breathing. There in the doorway, underneath a parka of rotten feathers, loomed a gaunt figure silhouetted in moonlight. Greasy, thinning hair dripped from its skull. Its menacing frame barely fit the doorway. Sharp, pointed fingers curved like blades from its hands. Frowning, it seemed ancient. Older than stars. The stench of seaweed and turned earth blew into the cabin. Slowly, it rotated its mutated shoulders and raised its arms into the moonlight. The daughter saw its fingernails glint, and between them, a fine loop of string curled. As those cold, bright eyes stared into her, an odd certainty dawned in her mind. It was him. The face from her dreams. The creature pulling her, dragging her underneath the ice. She saw the string laced between its tortured fingers and knew what she had done. She had awakened one of them. The Sleeping Ones. The Inuunngittut. The ones that drag you under. Slowly, a razor smile spread across the creature's face, each tooth gleaming wetly with delight. A deep, grating voice birthed in her skull.

"Child . . ."

Her eyes widened in disbelief. The creature spoke without speaking. It had growled in her mind and yet remained frozen. Its milky eyes studied her as its grin curdled into a horrid frown. The daughter felt the creature's mind reach out to her; its long, salivary thoughts moaned in satisfaction. Frozen in terror, her eyes fell to its parka. Mottled black and white, its rancid feathers stank of the lake. Its arms hung low—string laced between its fingers. Suddenly, the creature rushed toward her, violently shaking its head. White eyes screamed behind its frown. It stopped short before the daughter, sour breath heaving into her nostrils.

"P i c k . . . i t . . . u p . . ."

"What?" the girl whimpered. The creature lifted one long, twisted finger and dangled the string in front of her.

"C o n n n t e s s t . . ."

The daughter's eyebrows creased. Her shaking hand lifted and took the string. As she cradled it, something cackled in the back of her mind. The creature spread three long, bony fingers before her and nodded. Challenge. Best two out of three.

"Y o u . . . w i n . . . I . . . g o . . ." the creature growled into her mind. The daughter spun the string between her fingers. A murderous smile crept across the creature's face. *"I . . . w i n . . . y o u . . . g o . . ."*

"Go? Go where?!" Panic cracked the girl's voice. The creature lifted a nail to her face and traced a tear as it streaked down her cheek.

Her grandmother had told her stories. Stories of the Inuunngittut and the children who challenged them. It usually did not go well for the child. The daughter closed her eyes and thought of her mother, her grandmother, and the lives they had lived together. When she opened her eyes, the creature had retreated to the doorway. Its gangly arms slung low. A grin stitched across its face. "*C h o o s e . . .*" The daughter stared at the string between her fingers. She looked back at the creature and saw its ruffled feathers. Black speckled white. Loon's feathers. Something stirred in the depths of her mind and surfaced. Something her grandmother had told her.

"I choose Raven." The creature straightened its back. "My grandmother once told me a story. One her mother had told her. A story before colour. Raven and Loon." The creature's grin soured. Its eyes narrowed to razors. The daughter had struck a nerve. "Raven and Loon decided they no longer wanted to be colourless, right?" The girl started weaving her fingers. "So, Raven and Loon decided they wanted to paint one another. Raven went first and painted Loon so beautifully that in return Loon gave Raven some new *kamiik*." Anger twisted the creature's jaw as the daughter's fingers worked the story. "Raven was so thrilled with her kamiik that she could not stand still to be painted. Loon then became so angry that she poured the paint can all over Raven." The daughter raised a stringed Raven between her fingers and swayed it in the air. "Raven then flew away, a black bird in the sky." The creature then slowly raised its own bird framed in string. Second place. In a rage, the creature snapped its string and growled. The daughter's eyes widened as water trickled down the parka. The daughter unstrung her figure and turned to the creature. "Choose."

The creature raised its arms, string restored, and smiled in delight. The daughter met the creature's stare, and suddenly a word dredged through her mind.

"L a d d e r . . ."

The daughter's breath tightened in her chest. This figure she knew well, even with her eyes closed. It was a story her grandmother had learned when she was forced to go to school. A story from the Bible. Twin brothers. Jacob and Esau. Jacob had cheated his brother and, while fleeing, he fell asleep and dreamed of a ladder reaching between Heaven and Earth. Upon this ladder, angels ascended and descended between the two realms. God then promised Jacob that his people would spread like dust in the wind and that all the land would be theirs. A lesson befitting residential school. God could be an unrighteous bastard when he wanted to.

Suddenly in her mind, the daughter saw her grandmother as a little girl, far, far away from home. Scared and alone. Confused in a place of angels and demons. Of pain. Abandoned. Ripped from her family. Thrown to the winds. She paced the hallways with a deep sadness stitched to her heart. The daughter stood lifeless as she watched the creature's hands jerk and weave in patterns she'd never seen before. It was like watching a reflection in water. A celluloid negative, inverted and forgotten. She felt her mind fall, pirated by some errant, black signal. The static beyond worlds.

When she opened her eyes, she realized how hard they had been shut. Tears streamed down her face. When she looked at her hands, she realized her string lay still, prone in a ready position. She hadn't even started. She lifted her reddened eyes and felt a cackling in her mind. The creature's hideous grin loomed inches from her face. A finished ladder laced between its fingers. She gritted her teeth. "Y-You tricked me. You . . . showed me things!" Her swollen face betrayed her anger. The creature's voice reached out to her.

"Story..."

A puzzled look lingered over her. Story? Yes. She had told a story. Told it the same way it had been told to her and her mother before that. Raven and Loon. Victim and victor. The creature had done the same, channelled a story, breathed it into life. A story that had hit home, but a story all the same, despite how awful it may have been. She looked down at her unfinished figure. The creature stood ready, its outstretched arms strung together. The last figure of their contest. Loser's choice. The creature tilted its head back and uttered a deep, reptilian bellow. An ancient, resonating growl the daughter felt in the fillings of her teeth. The creature's monstrous weight sagged into the floorboards as it stepped forward. The daughter stepped back and rubbed her palms together. Despair crept into her fingers and knotted them. The air felt thick and syrupy. Suddenly, she could not breathe.

"Choose..."

Panic shut her eyes. She tried to steady her breathing. She tried not to think of creatures that should not be. She thought of her grandmother. She inhaled, and the scent of spruce boughs and wood smoke filled her mind. Flooded with memory, she remembered the safety of her grandmother's lap, watching storms weave between her fingers. The warmth of the memory spread through her and pushed everything else out of her mind. She could almost hear her grandmother's tales. Her whispered stories of animals that had existed long ago. Creatures that should not be. Excitement lit the daughter's face. She raised her hands and spoke a single word.

The creature stepped back. Its eyes narrowed to call her bluff. The daughter closed her eyes. She thought of her grandmother, her fingers looping and twisting. The daughter's hands began to ache. She looked down, surprised to see she had already begun. The creature quickly followed suit in its odd, jerking fashion. As she wove, the daughter paced step by step with the memory, yet confusion dogged her mind. She couldn't fully remember the pattern, the stringing of it lost in time. Her grandmother had had the same problem; the memory had faded over generations. Panicked, she looked to the creature, and its lifeless eyes stared right back into her. Without looking, its spidery fingers looped with conviction. It could spin gold if it wanted to. The daughter's confidence emptied. She could feel her line beginning to tangle. The creature had yet to miss a beat. She closed her eyes and thought of the story bridging her palms. Connecting worlds.

She is six years old. She is watching her anaanatsiaq's fingers loop and curl. She is telling her of a figure that has faded away like clouds in sunshine. She has trouble focusing. Memories ripple into waves. Her grandmother is trying to tell her to pay attention, but she is having trouble. Her mind keeps drifting away.

The daughter opened her eyes and saw that the creature had stopped as well. Its terrible frown studied her coldly. She closed her eyes again.

Her grandmother is trying to remember. Trying to recollect a figure her grandmother had taught her, and hers before that. Like a distant star growing farther with every generation, it is fading. Mammoth. A figure that should not exist. First strung when people lived alongside the huge ancient beasts. This fragment—this artifact— was the bridge. The ladder. It connected her to the past. To the infinite. Not the figure itself, but the act of it. A sense of belonging. An affirmation. The daughter opened her eyes as she felt her knuckles twist through the final loops.

Suddenly, her line caught. Her fingers itched and burned. She made to finish, but her string snagged and netted. She looked up at the creature and saw it hunched over, rasping perversely. Slowly, its malformed spine straightened while its clawed hands spread before her.

"*M a m m o t h . . . d e a d . . . G r a n d m o t h e r . . . d e a d . . .*" It slowly raised its head, and a hideous smile split the corners of its lips.

"*D a u g h t e r . . . d e a d . . .*"

The creature presented its figure, pulsing with horrid life. Black blood trickled down its string. Slicing into the creature's fingers, a clotted mammoth rode the moonlight. The creature's voice whispered in her mind.

"*D o w n . . . d o w n . . . d o w n . . .*"

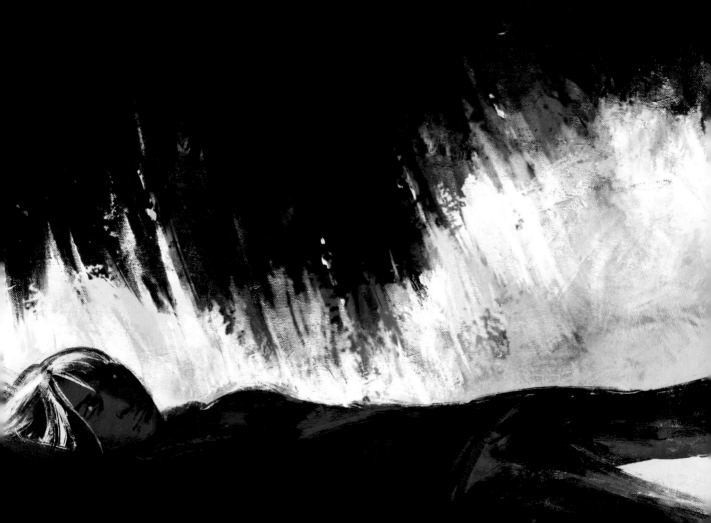

Static suddenly roared through the room, and the daughter became acutely aware that she could not move. Frozen, paralyzed. The creature's grin ran over her as its horrible body turned and lumbered out the doorway. Her body fell hard to the floor, and she could only watch as invisible strings dragged her out of the cabin and down the snowy trail to the lake. The creature walked with a patient gait while it pulled a feathered hood over its greasy skull.

As the two of them crossed onto open ice, the mother turned in her sleep. She felt as though an eerie fog had lifted and cleared. She sat up, half conscious, and realized it was much colder in the cabin than before. She groggily looked to the wide-open door and yawned. She rubbed her eyes and saw that, in fact, the door was missing. She squinted into the distance and made out what appeared to be two silhouettes walking to the lake. One walking and the other . . . sliding? The mother looked to her daughter's couch and saw it empty. The mother immediately got up and ran to the door. She saw the standing figure stop and turn its head. What she saw chilled her spine. Two horrible eyes glowed white underneath the hood. It raised an arm, and, with a flick of its wrist, the smooth lake ice cracked like broken glass. Deep fissures riddled the surface, and the mother watched as the figure slowly descended into the cold waters, dragging its cargo behind it with every step down. The mother recognized her daughter's long hair as it slid toward the broken ice. The mother sprinted toward the lake barefoot. The shocking cold welled tears in her eyes as she saw her daughter's rigid body slip into the water. As she ran, she watched her daughter's head turn, her pleading eyes calling out before finally rolling under.

As the mother neared the shore, she grabbed the ice chisel sticking out of one of the qamutiit. She saw the cracks in the ice begin to heal, becoming long, meandering scars over the lake. When she reached where she had seen her daughter slip under, it had just frozen over. She looked down through the ice and saw her daughter's outstretched hand fade into darkness. The mother brought the chisel down in hard, violent strikes. She screamed as frozen crystals flew up and stung her face. Hunks of murky ice broke off, and the faster she cut, the faster it grew back. The mother's swollen feet burned in slushy water as she cut deeper and deeper. Suddenly, a face was rising to meet her. Eager to free her child, she chipped harder, sensing her nearby. She saw her daughter's pearled eyes rising, her mouth gasping for air. Crying, the mother stabbed desperately as her daughter reached from the other side of the ice. She raised her spear and her eyes opened wide as she saw her daughter's small mouth suddenly frown viciously. Like an eel rushing toward the surface, the daughter's jaw flung wide, her teeth unforgiving, pointed, and curved. She reached out to her mother, her fingers webbed and fishlike. The daughter's eyes flashed into horrid silver dollars as the creature reached the surface, shrieking behind rows of teeth.

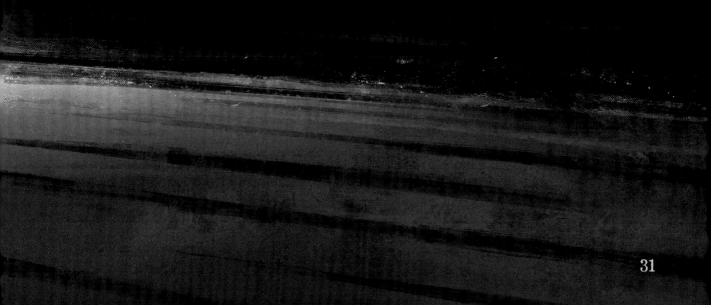

"HOLY SHIT!" the mother screamed as she plunged the chisel down in one explosive lunge. As it broke through the ice, the handle's string glided off her fingers as the chisel dug deep into the creature's throat, striking bone in one wet thud. The long, carved handle twitched and bobbed oddly as the creature gurgled and slowly sank into darkness. The chisel knocked against the sides of the chipped hole as it slipped under. The lake stopped freezing over, and the mother knelt and looked into the water. The creature left slow swirls in its wake as it sank to the bottom. Desperately, the mother immediately threw her arms into the water for any trace of her daughter. She cried and pleaded for her. In a shrill whisper, she prayed for her mother to help her. To help bring her baby back to her.

A single brown nub spun among the ice. A knot. The mother reached in, pulled, and felt something weighing it down. She pulled harder and saw small, slight fingers tangled in the sinew. She reached down and grabbed hold. Listless, the hand sagged under her grip. The mother's soul dropped, and she sobbed loudly as she continued to pull. Soon her daughter's sweet, round face appeared in the water, sunken and pale with cold, blue lips. She wailed to see her lifeless child.

As she began lifting her daughter's body through the ice, something stirred and jerked the girl down. Wide eyed and terrorized, the mother felt it pull again, yanking her into the chipped hole. The daughter's eyes suddenly burst open. Half in the icy water, mother and daughter thrashed to be free. The mother screamed as her face bobbed below the surface. Her knees twisted to find purchase on the ice. Her hands under her daughter's arms, the mother pulled and lifted her daughter's head above water. "MOMMY, IT'S GOT ME!" the daughter screamed. The mother's back strained as she tried to heave her daughter onto the ice.

"KICK, MY GIRL!" the mother bellowed as the daughter felt a clawed hand grip her ankle and pull her down. The daughter's face plunged below the surface, and she looked down to see those horrid white eyes staring back into her. She stomped her foot down into its face, and then, as quickly as mother and daughter had been pulled in, they were suddenly let go. The two crashed on the surface of the ice. The mother held her daughter in a heap. Soaked and freezing in the moonlit night, the two gasped for air. The daughter suddenly pushed her mother away and retched long, choking sobs before murky lake water finally burst out of her lungs. The mother then held her close and told her repeatedly that it was okay. It was all over. The creature was gone. Shaking, the daughter looked down at her trembling hands and saw the string laced between her fingers. She unravelled it and threw it into the chipped hole. It rested on the icy surface and then slowly sank, spiralling into the depths below. The daughter cried into her mother's arms, finally free. The moon burned coldly above. In the dark beneath the ice, the waters swelled, and, in the distance, a soft, wooden thudding faded into the night.

Taima.

Before Dawn

"Can I go out and play, Mom?" Simeonie pleaded.

"Okay. . . but no farther than the *inuksuk*, Sim."

Two boys leapt off the porch and ran. The land rolled out before them, from golden tundra to midday sun. In the distance, a lone inuksuk straddled the horizon, marking the borders of home. Pushing and tumbling over one another, the boys ran with the zeal of the newly freed. Hiding behind old cars and barrels, they peeked through their fingers and counted to ten.

They reached the inuksuk rosy cheeked and out of breath. Their shadows burned long and misshapen in the summer sun. Shielding their eyes, they stopped to catch their breath and gaze over the land. Hiding places had become sparse, so much so that Isaac pointed to the next hill.

"We should go over there!"

Simeonie turned to where Isaac pointed, but the sight of Isaac's teeth suddenly caught him off guard. There were too many of them. They curled inward behind his broad smile. Isaac squinted his eyes as he pointed to where he wanted to play. A bead of saliva slowly dribbled from his jagged grin, giving Simeonie pause.

". . . Mom said no farther than the inuksuk, Isaac."

"But look!" Isaac insisted, pointing to a rocky figure on the next hill. Having never seen it before, Simeonie rubbed his eyes in disbelief. Yet there it stood, as large as life and twice as natural.

"No farther than there, right? C'mon!" Isaac yelled as he pulled Simeonie into the distance.

Simeonie resisted at first, but soon his legs were kicking up dirt as he and Isaac laughed, sprinting out of bounds. As they ran, Isaac began to sing . . .

"If I could but learn to fly, but oh, my feet are turning into stone, Ayaya aya ya."

A vague sense of happiness washed over Simeonie. Smiling, he looked down as they hurried across the hills. He laughed. In eerie leaps and bounds, they rushed over the land. It spun beneath their feet, and with every landscape they crossed, another distant inuksuk tended the horizon. Simeonie thought, *What magic is this?*

When they finally came to a rest, Simeonie realized the day was beginning to fade. Darkness began to fill the sky and take root in the back of his mind. He quickly looked around for some landmark that could tell him where he was. Nothing seemed familiar.

"We need to go home, Isaac," Simeonie whimpered. Worry cracked his young voice.

Yet his friend stood silent, staring into the sun. He closed his eyes and breathed deeply to savour the moment. To remember.

"I'm going to miss you, Sim," Isaac finally confessed. He looked over the barrenlands and sighed. The last rays of daylight faded beneath the horizon. The dry shrubs and yellowing grass darkened to a pale grey. "I didn't bring you out here to play, Sim. I'm taking you away." Pain washed over Isaac's face. "I've taken so many before you. So many sacrifices. That one day I may be free. You will finally bring that day."

"Isaac, you're not making sense . . ."

"You were my favourite, Sim. I couldn't have asked for a better friend. I wish I had something better to give you." Isaac spread his arms to the horizon. "This eternal sunset is now yours, Sim. I can't take it anymore. Living between worlds is hard. Belonging neither to existence nor eternity, but with a foot in both." Isaac sighed; his breath faltered. "It gets lonely, Sim."

"Isaac, you're scaring—"

"My name isn't Isaac," the boy snapped bitterly. "If not for the look on people's faces, I wouldn't use that name. You know the look, the realization in a person's eyes that says, 'I should have known better.'" Isaac twisted and chuckled grimly, "Not *I-saac* but *I-ji-raq*!"

Simeonie's eyes widened in disbelief. *Ijirait* were said to be monsters, part of the Inuunngittut, the Others that take children and hide them away, forever lost and unfound. Simeonie's mother had warned of them, of strange people, or animals even, lest they should spirit you away. She had especially warned Simeonie about hide and seek. That was the ijiraq's speciality. Simeonie closed his eyes in pain. He should have known better. Isaac had been such a good friend, though. There was no way he could have known. Right?

Just as he thought this, the ijiraq's eyes turned black and lifeless. It stared blankly through Simeonie as if he wasn't even there. Its soulless eyes then cracked and splintered; deep flaws of red shone underneath. Its lips began to jerk and spasm grotesquely. Ancient syllables spat out of its mouth. Its face rippled, teeth turning in place. Simeonie heard the unmistakable crack of bone as hunks of flesh splattered to the ground. Twitching, the creature madly scuttled toward Simeonie and stopped just short of his face. Its fractured eyes peered behind bits of scalp. A vicious smile split vertically down the creature's face. Its sideways lips smacked over crowded teeth and giggled obscenely. Simeonie's stomach curdled. The ijiraq's crooked smile then spoke deeply, its gory lips careful to savour every syllable.

"If you are not home come morning, you will be as so many *inuksuit* before you. Lost . . . alone . . . " Slowly, the creature brought a misshapen hand to Simeonie's face. "I'll feed and fatten on your light and be free." It licked its lips and grinned horribly. "Then no more talk of you and me."

Simeonie tore his gaze away. In the distance, he recognized the stone cairn cresting the horizon. Suddenly, the creature's warm breath hissed into his ear.

"Run, boy. Run home to Mommy."

Its hideous lips quivered with delight as it taunted, "She's scared and she's crying, Sim." Its eyebrows furrowed, mocking care.

The image of his mother triggered something inside of Simeonie. In his mind, he pictured his mother distraught and hurt. It stirred the pit of his stomach and struck home.

Simeonie ran. He ran and he ran, and he felt the creature tittering into his ears behind every step. After what seemed to be an eternity, Simeonie stopped to catch his breath, horrified to see he had only made it to the first inuksuk. *Impossible*, he thought.

There are still so many! How did we come so far so fast? He placed a hand on the inuksuk's leg and felt a faint memory echo through the stone and escape his lips.

"If only I could find my way home, but oh, my feet are turning into stone, Ayaya aya ya."

In the distance, the ijiraq smiled repulsively, urging him on with dead eyes. As Simeonie sang its song, perverse satisfaction lit the ijiraq's face.

"Yes, child." Its upright smile drooled. "Sing."

Simeonie rose to his feet. His heart lifted, and a smile spread across his face. He worked his legs and realized that the more he sang, the more he bounded across the land. But a sick dread began to fill his heart as he realized—summer nights are not long in the North.

Inuksuit rose and fell beneath his feet. Hills and barrenlands swept away. Yet, as the sky filled with light, the first hint of dawn

weighed heavily upon Simeonie. He sang again, phrases forming from thin air.

"*Oh, my legs are turning into stone, Ayaya aya ya.*"

Finally, Simeonie reached the inuksuk where it had all begun. The first one. He had made it home. He screamed out as the sun crept over the ridge and pierced the sky with its brilliance.

"Mommy!"

Simeonie's mother ripped open the door. Her long, sleepless night had left her jumping at every start. But this time she swore she had heard her son cry. She surveyed the inuksuk hill for the thousandth time and momentarily felt the pall of dread lift from her heart.

Silhouetted by the dawn, a small figure stood beside the large inuksuk. She smiled and wiped the tears running down her face. Straining against the sudden morning light, she brought a hand to her face to shield her eyes and see her boy. But when her eyes adjusted, she found not her son but a small pillar of stones, stacked one on top of the other, standing beside the large inuksuk. Heartbroken, she gazed, mute and in disbelief. *Had it always been there?*

Realizing her son was not about to breach the horizon, she fell to the ground. In abandoned sobs, she broke down and begged and pleaded for her child. When there was nothing left to scream, she was silent, like so much rubble before the dawn.

Taima.

Glossary of Inuktut Words

Inuktut is the word for Inuit languages spoken in Canada, including Inuktitut and Inuinnaqtun. The pronunciation guides in this book are intended to support non-Inuktut speakers in their reading of Inuktut words. These pronunciations are not exact representations of how the words are pronounced by Inuktut speakers.

For more resources on how to pronounce Inuktut words, visit inhabitmedia.com/inuitnipingit.

Term	Pronunciation	Meaning
anaanatsiaq	ah-NAH-naht-see-ahk	grandmother
ijiraq	ee-YEE-rahk	a shadow person
ijirait	ee-YEE-rah-eet	shadow people
inuksuit	ee-NOOK-shoo-eet	plural of inuksuk
inuksuk	ee-NOOK-shook	rock cairn used to aid hunters and indicate direction
Inuunngittut	ee-NOO-ngee-toot	name for the Other Ones, creatures from Inuit traditional stories
kamiik	kah-MEEK	a pair of skin boots
qamutiit	KAH-moo-teet	sleds
taima	TAH-ee-mah	the end
ulu	OO-loo	crescent knife traditionally used by women

Jamesie Fournier

An Inuk raised in Denendeh, Jamesie Fournier's work has appeared in *Inuit Art Quarterly*, *Red Rising* magazine, *Northern Public Affairs*, and the anthology *Coming Home: Stories from the Northwest Territories*. His brother, Zebede Tulugaq Evaluardjuk-Fournier, illustrated his last two projects with *Inuit Art Quarterly*. Jamesie was guest author at the 2018 and 2020 Northwords Writers Festivals and a runner-up for the 2018 Sally Manning Award for Indigenous Creative Non-Fiction. He lives in Thebacha/Fort Smith between Salt River First Nation, Smith's Landing First Nation, and the South Slave Métis Nation.

Toma Feizo Gas

Toma Feizo Gas has spent ten years working in entertainment arts, with experience in production art, creative direction, concept design, and illustration.